ATOMIC ACE
(He's Just My Dad)

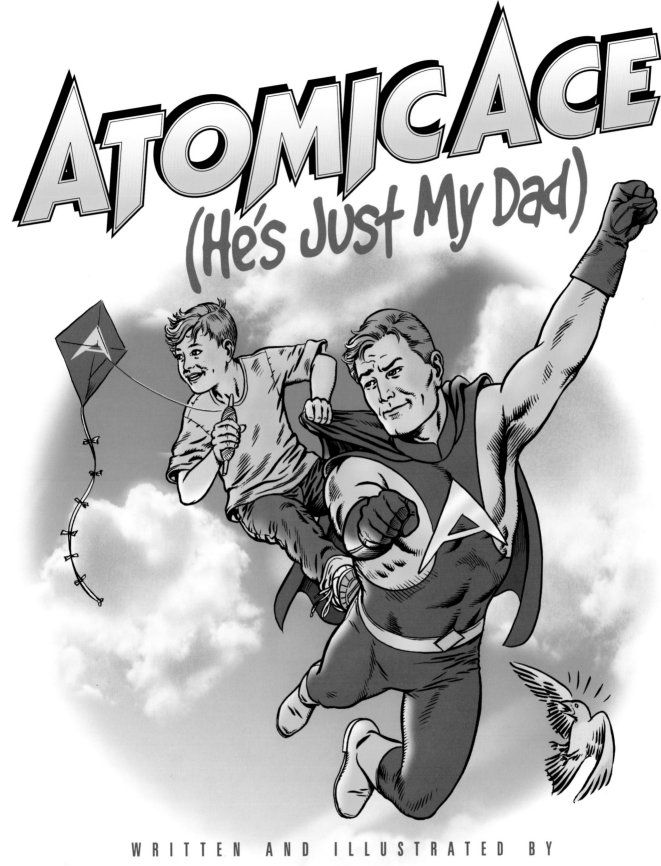

WRITTEN AND ILLUSTRATED BY
JEFF WEIGEL

Albert Whitman & Company
Morton Grove, Illinois

Library of Congress Cataloging-in-Publication Data

Weigel, Jeff, 1958-
Atomic Ace : (he's just my dad) / written and illustrated by Jeff Weigel.
p. cm.
Summary: In this rhyming story told in comic book format, a boy considers his family normal, though
his superhero dad, Atomic Ace, does amazing feats, even battling the evil Insect King.
ISBN 0-8075-3216-9 (hardcover)   ISBN 0-8075-3217-7 (paperback)
[1. Fathers and sons—Fiction. 2. Heroes—Fiction. 3. Cartoons and comics. 4. Stories in rhyme.] I. Title.
PZ8.3.W418 At 2004   [E]—dc22   2003017523

The line illustrations in this book were produced with ink and brush on bristol board.
Artwork was then scanned and coloring was done electronically in Adobe Photoshop on an Apple Mac G4 Cube.
The book was designed by the author and assembled in QuarkXpress.

For more information about Albert Whitman & Company,
please visit our web site: www.albertwhitman.com.

For Mom and Dad

"It must be so cool to live at your place!"

When friends tell me this, I can't keep a straight face!

They don't seem to get it. Sure, Dad battles crime,

but our lives are still average. (Well, most of the time!)

I do my homework while Mom makes us supper.

My dad might sweep up—he's a good cleaner-upper.

At dinner we talk and Dad maybe will say,

"I nabbed some bank robbers. How was your day?"

My family is normal. That's not so bad—

Mom's just my mom and Dad's just my dad.

Life with my dad's not as strange as it seems.

So the guy fights with robots and stops evil schemes!

He's always at home for our Saturday lunch.

He fixes my favorite—hot dogs and punch.

Yeah, some kids would say it *is* a big deal,

the unusual way Dad cooks us a meal.

But the stuff he heats up is easy to fix,

like French fries and burgers or frozen fish sticks.

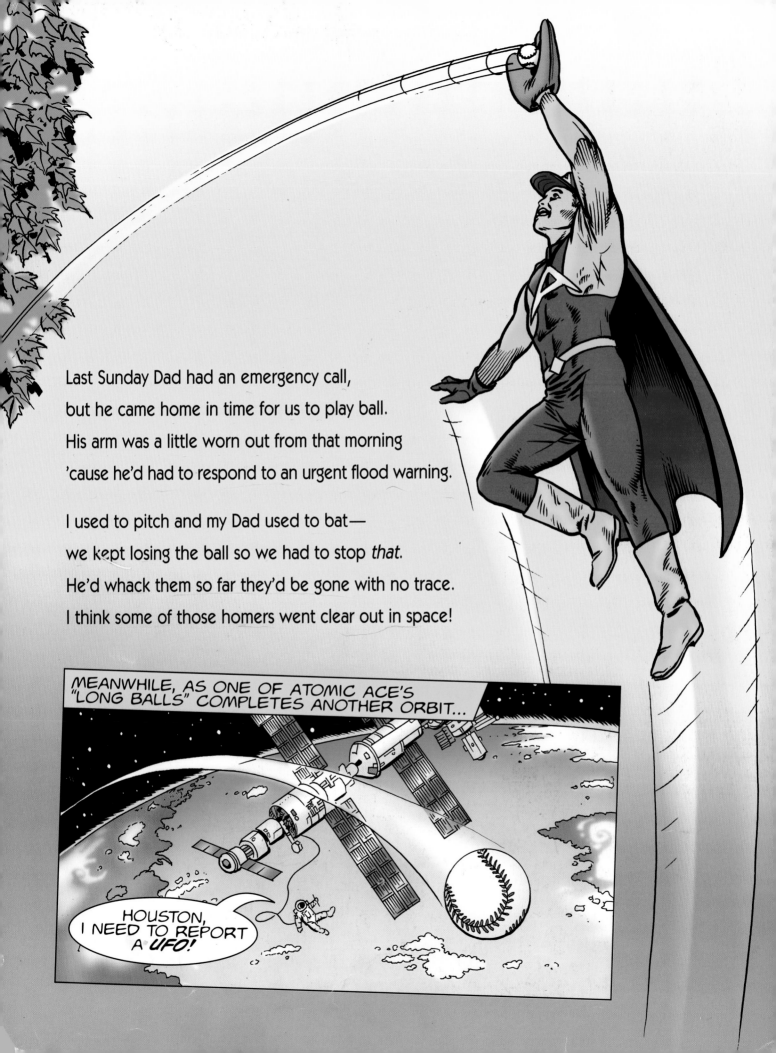

Last Sunday Dad had an emergency call,
but he came home in time for us to play ball.
His arm was a little worn out from that morning
'cause he'd had to respond to an urgent flood warning.

I used to pitch and my Dad used to bat—
we kept losing the ball so we had to stop *that*.
He'd whack them so far they'd be gone with no trace.
I think some of those homers went clear out in space!

MEANWHILE, AS ONE OF ATOMIC ACE'S "LONG BALLS" COMPLETES ANOTHER ORBIT...

HOUSTON, I NEED TO REPORT A *UFO!*

But some kids in my class don't see Dad my way.
They don't think he's normal, despite what I say.
Like the day Chad and Mike got all nasty and mean
over whose dad caught the biggest fish ever seen.

Then I said, "Hey, guys, my dad fishes, too!
He just gave a big one to the city's new zoo."
My friends overheard me; they seemed real impressed,
and one of them said, "Wow! Your dad's the best!"
But Chad made a face, and Mike kind of sneered;
then Chad whispered to Mike, "His dad's really weird!"

Dad's been busy these days—there's a tough case at work.

Some guy dressed in a bug suit is being a jerk.

When the city's in trouble Dad's always on hand,

but I stay busy, too—I just joined the school band!

My very first concert was coming up soon.

Would I do okay? Would I play in tune?

Dad told me, "Relax—I know you'll do fine,"

as he tucked me in bed at the usual time.

"Don't fret about things that others might say.

If you just do your best, you'll be more than okay!"

My dad never worries about looking bad.

Sure—folks think *he's* great. But *I'm* not my dad.

The night of the concert I had to dress up.

I was still kinda worried that I might mess up.

Mom told me that Dad called; he had to work late.

He said that he'd try to be finished by eight.

The band room was full. Mom was in the first row.
But the seat for my dad was still empty. *Oh, no!*
I was pretty annoyed that Dad wasn't there.
I knew he was working, but didn't he care?

Once the concert began, I soon stopped feeling mad.
The show went pretty well! Hey, we didn't sound bad!

Dad was at home when we came back that night,
and when we first saw him we got quite a fright!
His day hadn't gone well; he seemed sorta stressed.
In fact, worse than that—he seemed really depressed!

Dad said he was sorry. I said, "It's okay."
(I know what it feels like to have an off day.)
"Nobody's perfect," Mom said with a sigh.
Sometimes Dad messes up, but we still love the guy.

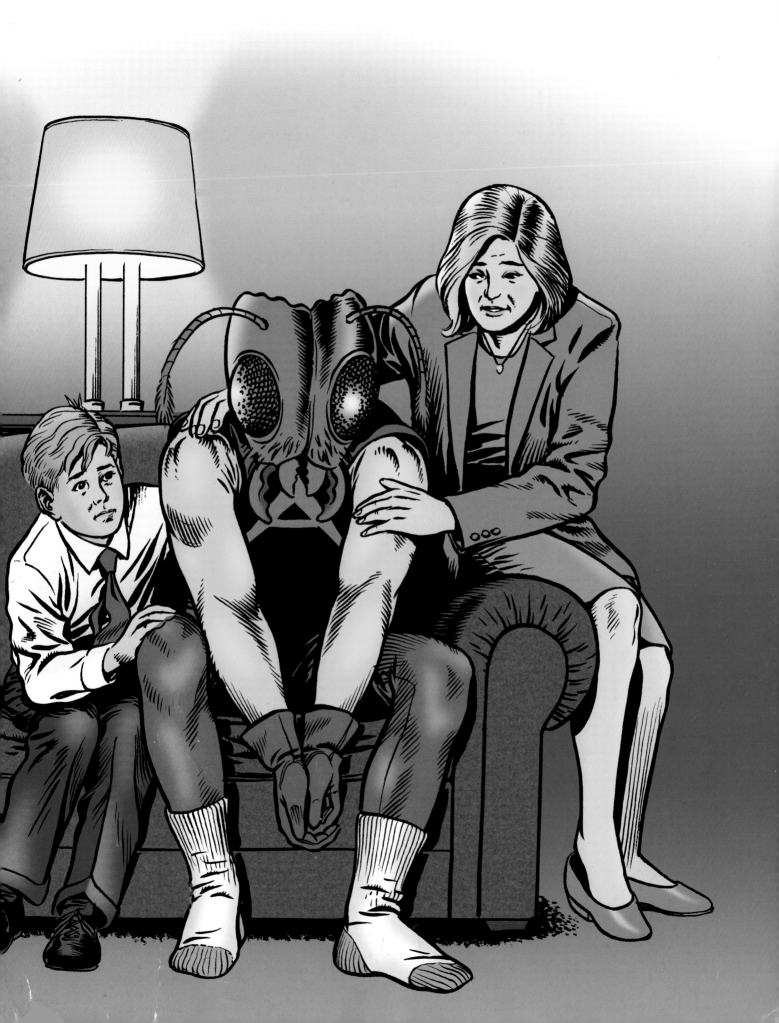

Dad wasn't himself for the next couple days.
He just hates it when bad guys zap him with rays!
Like that time he came home shrunk to six inches tall—
our cat tried to eat him right there in our hall!

As the weekend went on, he got gradually better—
just waiting things out in his old comfy sweater.
He looked pretty weird with the face that he had,
but ant-head or not, he was still my dad.

Dad seemed his old self when Monday began.

All weekend long he'd been hatching a plan.

He flew off to work as I got on the bus.

When the other kids saw him, they raised quite a fuss!

They'd heard what had happened to Dad on the news.

"Did he fight Insect King?! Did he actually *lose?!*"

The questions they asked made me feel sort of mad!

I said, "Mind your own business! After all, he's *my dad.*"

When I went into school, I got even more steamed;

those creeps Mike and Chad were especially mean!

"Wanna go on a picnic? Your dad might crawl by!"

I wanted to sock 'em...and I almost did try!

But my folks always tell me never to fight

('less the world is at stake and you're fighting for right!).

But later that day some good news had spread:
"Insect King Captured!" the newspapers read.
At dinner Dad had a good story to tell,
and we heard how his troubles turned out pretty well.
We were eating our burgers and having a laugh
when *Chad* came up asking for Dad's autograph!

We were happy to see Dad's good spirits were back,

so I thought I'd make popcorn—his favorite snack.

We got ready for bed, we watched some TV,

then we all sat around—my mom, Dad, and me.

I have to admit Dad's not like other guys:

he's got nuclear powers, and sometimes he flies!

He takes trips to space, and he's been to Earth's core!

He's done some cool stuff, and I'm sure he'll do more.

My dad conquers evil; my dad saves the day;

but he's still just my dad—and I like it that way.

To grow up just like Dad would really be fun,

and you know what they say—like father, like son!

E
WEI

Weigel, Jeff.

Atomic Ace.

Gr 2-3

$15.95

39545000706936